James, the Red Engine

THE REV. W. AWDRY

WITH ILLUSTRATIONS BY
C. REGINALD DALBY

RANDOM HOUSE NEW YORK

Britt Allcroft's Thomas & Friends based on The Railway Series by The Rev W Awdry
Copyright © Britt Allcroft (Thomas) LLC 1998
All rights reserved
THOMAS & FRIENDS is a trademark of Britt Allcroft Inc in the USA, Mexico, and Canada
and of Britt Allcroft (Thomas) Limited in the rest of the world
THE BRITT ALLCROFT COMPANY is a trademark of The Britt Allcroft Company plc
Published in the United States of America by Random House, Inc., New York, and simultaneously
in Canada by Random House of Canada Limited, Toronto.
Originally published in Great Britain in 1948 as Book 3 in The Railway Series.
First published in this edition in Great Britain in 1998 by Egmont Children's Books Limited.
Library of Congress Catalog Card Number: 99-62602   ISBN 0-375-80531-1
Printed in Mexico March 2000   10 9 8 7 6 5 4 3
www.randomhouse.com/kids
www.thomasthetankengine.com
RANDOM HOUSE and colophon are registered trademarks of Random House, Inc.

DEAR FRIENDS OF EDWARD, GORDON, HENRY, AND THOMAS,

Thank you for your kind letters. Here is the new book for which you asked.

James, who crashed into the story of *Thomas the Tank Engine,* settles down and becomes a useful engine.

We are nationalized now, but the same engines still work the Region. I am glad, too, to tell you that Sir Topham Hatt, who understands our friends' ways, is still in charge.

I hope you will enjoy this book, too.

THE AUTHOR

James and the Top-Hat

James was a new engine who lived at a station at the other end of the line. He had two small wheels in front and six driving wheels behind. They weren't as big as Gordon's, and they weren't as small as Thomas.'

"You're a special mixed-traffic engine," Sir Topham Hatt told him. "You'll be able to pull coaches or freight cars quite easily."

But freight cars are not easy things to manage, and on his first day they had pushed him down a hill into a field.

He had been ill after the accident, but now he had new brakes and a shining coat of red paint.

"The red paint will cheer you up after your accident," said Sir Topham Hatt kindly. "You are to pull coaches today, and Edward shall help you."

They went together to find the coaches.

"Be careful with the coaches, James," said Edward. "They don't like being bumped. Freight cars are silly and noisy—they need to be bumped and taught to behave— but coaches get cross and will get you back."

They took the coaches to the platform and were
both coupled on in front. Sir Topham Hatt, the

Stationmaster, and some little boys all came to admire James' shining rods and red paint.

James was pleased. "I am a really splendid engine," he thought, and suddenly let off steam. "*Whee—ee—ee—ee—eesh!*"

Sir Topham Hatt, the Stationmaster, and the Guard all jumped, and a shower of water fell on Sir Topham Hatt's nice new top hat.

Just then, the whistle blew, and James thought they had better go—so they went!

"Go on, go on," he puffed to Edward.

"Don't push, don't push," puffed Edward, for he did not like starting quickly.

"Don't go so fast, don't go so fast," grumbled the coaches, but James did not listen. He wanted to run away before Sir Topham Hatt could call him back.

He didn't even want to stop at the first station. Edward tried hard to stop, but the two coaches in front were beyond the platform before they stopped, and they had to go back to let the passengers get out.

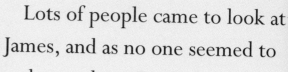

Lots of people came to look at James, and as no one seemed to know about Sir Topham Hatt's top hat, James felt happier.

Presently, they came to the junction where Thomas was waiting with his two coaches.

"Hello, James!" said Thomas kindly. "Feeling better? That's good.

Ah! That's my Guard's whistle. I must go. Sorry I can't stay. I don't know what Sir Topham Hatt would do without me to run this branch line." And he puffed off importantly with his two coaches into a tunnel.

Leaving the junction, they passed the field where James had had his accident. The fence was mended, and the cows were back again. James whistled, but they paid no attention.

They clattered through Edward's station yard and started to climb the hill beyond.

"It's ever so steep, it's ever so steep," puffed James.

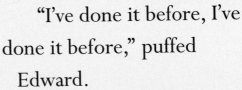

"I've done it before, I've done it before," puffed Edward.

"It's steep, but we'll do it—it's steep, but we'll do it," the two engines puffed together as they pulled the train up the big hill.

They both rested at the next station. Edward told James how Gordon had been stuck on the hill and he had had to push him up!

James laughed so much that he got hiccups and surprised an old lady in a black bonnet.

She dropped all her parcels, and three porters, the Stationmaster, and the Guard had to run after her, picking them up!

James was quiet in the shed that night. He had enjoyed his day, but he was a little afraid of what Sir Topham Hatt would say about the top hat!

James and the Bootlace

Next morning, Sir Topham Hatt spoke severely to James: "If you can't behave, I shall take away your red coat and have you painted blue."

James did not like that at all, and he was very rough with the coaches as he brought them to the platform.

"Come along, come along," he called rudely.

"All in good time, all in good time," the coaches grumbled.

"Don't talk, come on!" answered James, and with the

coaches squealing and grumbling after him, he snorted
into the station

James *was* cross that morning. Sir Topham Hatt had spoken to him, the coaches had dawdled, and worst of all, he had had to fetch his own coaches.

"Gordon never does," thought James, "and he is only painted blue. A splendid red engine like me should never have to fetch his own coaches." And he puffed and snorted around to the front of the train and backed up to it with a rude bump.

"O—ooooh!" groaned the coaches. "That was so bad!"

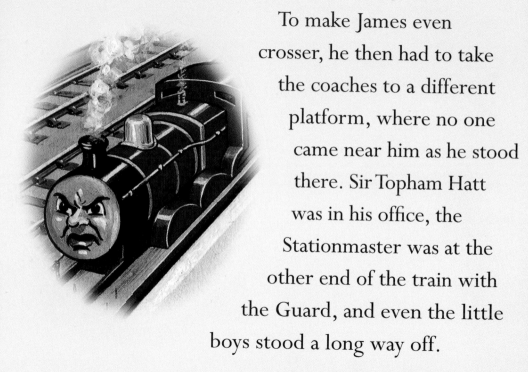

To make James even crosser, he then had to take the coaches to a different platform, where no one came near him as he stood there. Sir Topham Hatt was in his office, the Stationmaster was at the other end of the train with the Guard, and even the little boys stood a long way off.

James felt lonely. "I'll show
them!" he said to himself.
"They think Gordon is the
only engine who can
pull coaches."
And as soon
as the Guard's
whistle blew, he
started off with a tremendous jerk.

"Come on!—come on!—come on!" he puffed, and the coaches, squeaking and groaning in protest, clattered over the switches to the open line.

"Hurry!—hurry!—hurry!" puffed James.

"You're going too fast, you're going too fast," said the coaches, and indeed they were going so fast that they swayed from side to side.

James laughed and tried to go faster, but the coaches wouldn't let him.

"We're going to stop—we're going to stop—we're—going—to—stop," they said, and James found himself going slower and slower.

"What's the matter?" James asked his Driver.

"The brakes are on—leak in the pipe, most likely. You've banged the coaches enough to make a leak in anything."

The Guard and the Driver got down and looked at the brake pipes all along the train.

At last they found a hole where rough treatment had made a joint work loose.

"How shall we mend it?" said the Guard.

James' Driver thought for a moment.

"We'll do it with newspapers and a leather bootlace."

"Well, where is the bootlace coming from?" asked the Guard. "We haven't got one."

"Ask the passengers," said the Driver.

So the Guard made everyone get out.

"Has anybody got a leather bootlace?" he asked.

They all said, "No," except one man in a bowler hat (whose name was Jeremiah Jobling) who tried to hide his feet.

"You have a leather bootlace there, I see, sir," said the Guard. "Please give it to me."

"I won't," said Jeremiah Jobling.

"Then," said the Guard sternly, "I'm afraid this train will just stay where it is."

Then the passengers all told the Guard, the Driver, and the Fireman what a bad railway it was. But the Guard climbed into his car, and the Driver and the Fireman made James let off steam. So they all told Jeremiah Jobling he was a bad man instead.

At last, he gave them his laces, the Driver tied a pad of newspapers tightly around the hole, and James was able to pull the train.

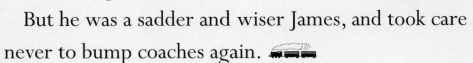

But he was a sadder and wiser James, and took care never to bump coaches again.

Troublesome Trucks

James did not see Sir Topham Hatt for several days. They left James alone in the shed, and did not even allow him to go out and push coaches and freight cars in the Yard.

"Oh, dear!" he thought sadly. "I'll never be allowed out anymore. I shall have to stay in this shed for always, and no one will ever see my red coat again. Oh, dear! Oh, dear!" James began to cry.

Just then, Sir Topham Hatt came along.

"I see you are sorry, James," he said. "I hope now that you will be a better engine. You have given me a lot of trouble. People are laughing at my railway, and I do not like that at all."

"I am very sorry, sir," said James. "I will try hard to behave."

"That's a good engine," said Sir Topham Hatt kindly. "I want you to pull some freight cars for me. Run along and find them."

So James puffed happily away.

"Here are your freight cars, James," said a little tank
engine. "Have you got some bootlaces ready?" And he ran
off, laughing rudely.

"Oh! Oh! Oh!" said the freight cars as James backed up to them. "We want a proper engine, not a red monster."

James took no notice and started as soon as the Guard was ready.

"Come along, come along," he puffed.

"We won't! We won't!" screamed the freight cars.

But James didn't care, and he pulled the screeching freight cars sternly out of the Yard.

The freight cars tried hard to make him give up, but he still kept on.

Sometimes their brakes would slip on, and sometimes their axles would "run hot." Each time they would have to stop and put the trouble right, and each time James would start again, determined not to let the freight cars beat him.

"Give up! Give up! You can't pull us! You can't! You can't!" called the freight cars.

"I can and I will! I can and I will!" puffed James.

And slowly but surely, he pulled them along the line.

At last, they saw Gordon's hill ahead.

"Look out for trouble, James," warned his Driver. "We'll go fast and get them up before they know it. Don't let them stop you."

So James went faster, and they were soon halfway up the hill.

"I'm doing it! I'm doing it!" he panted.

But it was hard work.

"Will the top never come?" he thought, when with a sudden jerk it all became easier.

"I've done it! I've done it!" he puffed triumphantly.

"Hurrah!" he thought. "It's easy now." But his Driver
shut off steam.

"They've done it again," he said. "We've left our tail behind!"

The last ten freight cars were running backward down the hill. The coupling had snapped!

But the Guard was brave. Very carefully and cleverly he made them stop. Then he got out and walked down the line with his red flag.

"That's why it was easy," said James as he backed the other freight cars carefully down. "What silly things freight cars are! There might have been an accident."

Meanwhile, the Guard had stopped Edward, who was pulling three coaches.

"Shall I help you, James?" called Edward.

"No, thank you," answered James, "I'll pull them myself."

"Good. Don't let them beat you."

So James got ready. Then with a *"peep peep,"* he was off.

"I *can* do it, I *can* do it," he puffed. He pulled and puffed as hard as he could.

"Peep pip peep peep! You're doing well!" whistled Edward as James slowly struggled up the hill, with clouds of smoke and steam pouring from his funnel.

"I've done it, I've done it," he panted, and disappeared over the top.

They reached their station safely. James was resting in the yard when Edward puffed by with a cheerful *"peep peep."*

Then, walking toward him across the rails, James saw...Sir Topham Hatt!

"Oh, dear! What will he say?" he asked himself sadly.

But Sir Topham Hatt was smiling. "I was in Edward's train and saw everything," he said. "You've made the most troublesome freight cars on the line behave. After that, you deserve to keep your red coat."

James and the Express

S ometimes Gordon and Henry slept in James' shed, and they would talk of nothing but bootlaces! James would talk about engines who got shut up in tunnels and stuck on hills, but they wouldn't listen and went on talking and laughing.

"You talk too much, little James," Gordon would say. "A fine strong engine like me has something to talk about. I'm the only engine who can pull the Express. When I'm not there, they need two engines. Think of that!"

"I've pulled expresses for years and have never once lost my way. I seem to know the right line by instinct," said Gordon proudly. Every wise engine knows, of course, that the Signalman works the switches to make engines run on the right lines, but Gordon was so proud that he had forgotten.

"Wake up, James," he said
the next morning. "It's
nearly time for the
Express. What are you
doing? Odd jobs? Ah,
well! We all have to
begin somewhere,
don't we? Run along
and get my coaches—
don't be late now."

James went to get Gordon's coaches. They were now all shining with lovely new paint. He was careful not to bump them, and they followed him smoothly into the station, singing happily. "We're going away, we're going away."

"I wish I was going with you," said James. "I would love to pull the Express and go flying along the line."

He left them in the station and went back to the Yard just as Gordon, with much noise and blowing of steam, backed up to the train.

Sir Topham Hatt was on the train with other important people, and as soon as they heard the Guard's whistle, Gordon started.

"Look at me now! Look at me now!" he puffed, and the coaches glided after him out of the station.

"*Poop poop poo poo poop!*—Good-bye, little James! See you tomorrow."

James watched the train disappear around a curve and then went back to work. He pushed some freight cars into their proper sidings and went to fetch the coaches for another train.

He brought the coaches to the platform and was just being uncoupled when he heard a mournful, quiet *"Shush shush shush shush!"*

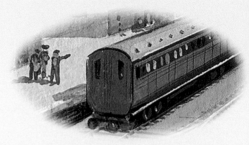

And there was Gordon, trying to sidle into the station without being noticed.

"Hello, Gordon! Is it tomorrow?" asked James.

Gordon didn't answer. He just let off
steam feebly.

"Did you lose your way, Gordon?"

"No, it was lost for me," he
answered crossly. "I was
switched off the Main
Line onto the loop. I had to go all
around and back again."

"Perhaps it was instinct," said
James brightly.

Meanwhile, all the passengers hurried to the ticket office. "We want our money back," they shouted.

Everyone was making noise, but Sir Topham Hatt climbed on a trolley and blew the Guard's whistle so loudly that they all stopped to look at him.

Then he promised them a new train at once.

"Gordon can't do it," he said. "Will you pull it for us, James?"

"Yes, sir, I'll try."

So James was coupled on, and everyone got in again.

"Do your best, James," said Sir Topham Hatt kindly. Just then, the whistle blew, and he had to run to get in.

"Come along, come along," puffed James.

"You're pulling us well! You're pulling us well," sang the coaches.

"Hurry, hurry, hurry," puffed James.

Stations and bridges flashed by, the passengers leaned out of the windows and cheered, and they soon reached the terminus.

Everyone said, "Thank you" to James.

"Well done," said Sir Topham Hatt. "Would you like to pull the Express sometimes?"

"Yes, please," answered James happily.

The next day when James came by, Gordon was pushing freight cars in the Yard.

"I like some quiet work for a change," he said. "I'm teaching these freight cars manners. You did well with those coaches, I hear... Good, we'll show them!" And he gave his freight cars a bump, making them cry, "Oh! Oh! Oh! Oh!"

James and Gordon are now good friends. James sometimes takes the Express to give Gordon a rest. Gordon never talks about bootlaces, and they are both quite agreed on the subject of freight cars!

TITLES IN
THE RAILWAY SERIES